Remembering Pat O'Hanlon
SG

In memory of Mum and Dad,
and with love to Gerry for
all her support
MO

Library of Congress-in-Publication Data Available

10   9   8   7   6   5   4   3   2   1

Published in 2004 by Sterling Publishing Co., Inc.
387 Park Avenue South, New York, NY 10016
First published in 2004 in Great Britain by
LITTLE TIGER PRESS
An imprint of Magi Publications
1 The Coda Centre, 189 Munster Road, London SW6 6AW
www.littletigerpress.com
Published in Canada by Sterling Publishing Company
C/o Canadian Manda Group, One Atlantic Avenue
Suite 105, Toronto, Ontario, Canada M6K 3E7
Text copyright © Sally Golding 2004
Illustrations copyright © Mark Oliver 2004

Printed in Dubai

Sterling ISBN 1-4027-1364-9

Foley and Jem

Sally Golding   Mark Oliver

Sterling Publishing Co., Inc.
New York

Jem was just like any dog:
handsome, brave, and full-hearted.
He lived with his friend, Foley.
They were very happy.
Jem loved Foley, and Foley
loved Jem.

Foley also loved the stars. He
read about the planets and the
universe and black holes.
Sometimes he read a book
about Earth, just for Jem.

At night Foley watched the
stars. Jem sat by him, his head in
Foley's lap. He gazed at Foley,
and Foley gazed at the stars.

"Good dog, good dog," Foley
said, patting Jem's head.

At Christmas, Jem gave Foley a star on a string.

"This is the best present you could give me," said Foley.

"Because it's given me a great idea."

"Imagine going into space," said Foley.

"What a strange idea," thought Jem.

But Foley went ahead with the plans and calculations. He worked hard.

It took him months to build it . . .

...the first **ever**
rocket for dogs!

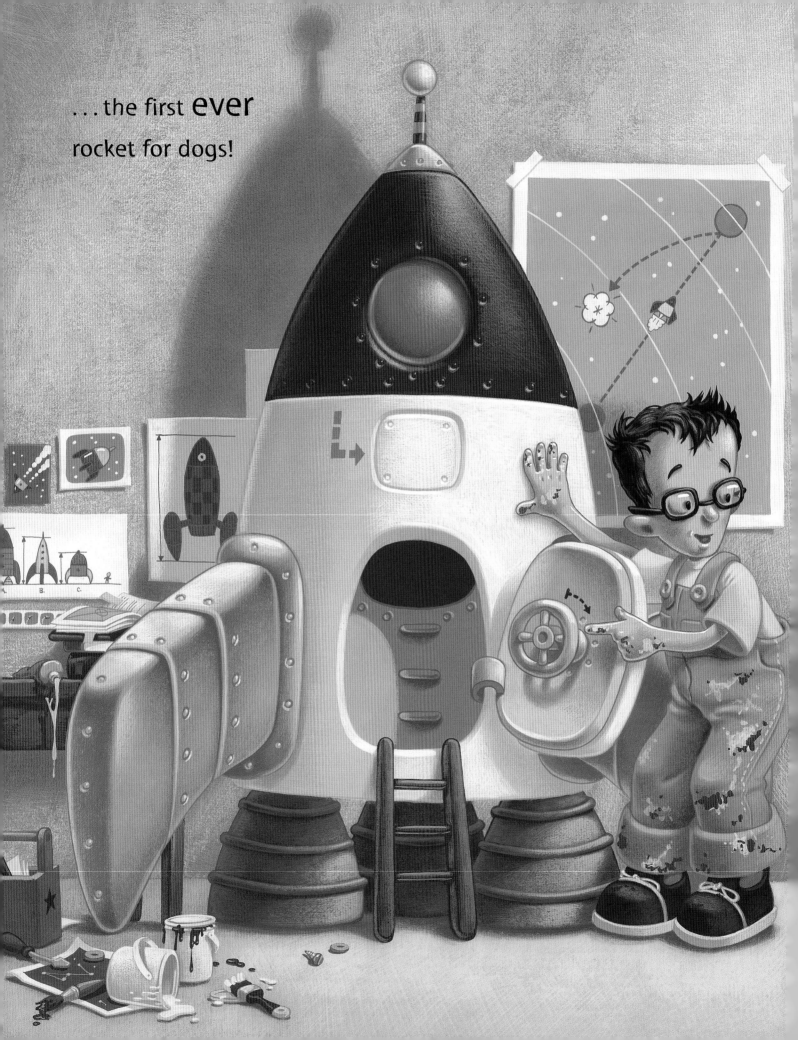

Foley's rocket would go all the way into space and land on Mars.

"This is fantastic, Jem!" exclaimed Foley. "Imagine exploring Mars! I wish I could go in the rocket, but I need to control things from Earth," said Foley.

"You can go, Jem. It will be a giant leap for dog-kind."

Foley made a special spacesuit
for Jem. Jem learned all the
rocket controls.

"I'll miss Foley on my trip," thought Jem. "But he'll miss me too. No one fetches sticks as well as I do. And no one knows how to keep Foley's feet warm in bed either. And who will bark when he comes home from school?"

Foley was too excited to remember the sticks and chilly feet and barking. He could only gaze out his window and wonder about Jem's great adventure.

The next day was launch day. The rocket shimmered in the sun. Lots of people cheered, and a brass band played.

The countdown started.

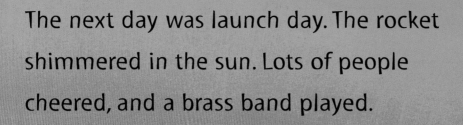

Ten! Nine! Eight!

"Here we go!" said Foley, looking at his rocket.

Seven! Six! Five!

Foley squinted to see Jem in the rocket window.

Four! Three!

"See you soon, Jem!" said Foley. Suddenly, he was very sad.

Two! One!

BLAST OFF!

The rocket rose
into the air.

"Goodbye, Earth!" said Jem, alone in the rocket.
Space felt strange and empty and lonely...
but beautiful and exciting as well. Jem
was surprised.

"This is interesting. No wonder Foley loves it."
He used the special camera to send pictures
back to Foley.

That night Foley thought of Jem and watched the sky.

"Good dog," he said, patting his knee where Jem's head usually rested. He felt a bony knee instead of a warm, silky head.

"Time for bed," said Foley.

The bed felt strange and empty. And lonely.

Jem landed the rocket
safely on Mars. He sent a message:

ARRIVED SAFELY.

He did everything properly, just like any
dog would. Mars was full of rocks and cracks
and sand. Jem sent pictures to Foley.
"Not much at all," Foley said. "It looks
like our driveway."

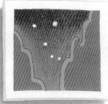

But the next day Jem walked all the way
to the other side of Mars.

What a sight!

"Hello," said the Martians.

"Hello," said Jem. They understood each other.

"Welcome to Mars, Earthling," they said.

Jem could breathe Martian air without his spacesuit. "This is even better than Earth!" he said.

Jem was too busy to send any pictures to Foley that day.

The next day, Foley sent
a message to Jem.

I MISS YOU, PLEASE SEND PICTURES
OF YOUR FRIENDLY FACE,

Jem put on his spacesuit
and sent this picture
and message:

I'M HAPPY HERE,
DON'T WORRY, HOPE YOU
ARE WELL,

"He's having all this fun without me," thought Foley. "Jem should be here with me fetching sticks, and warming my feet, and barking when I get home."

Foley looked at the photo sadly and wondered how long Jem's trip would last.

Each night Foley looked up at the
stars. But he wasn't excited
anymore. He was hoping to see
the rocket returning home.

One night while he was waiting for Jem, a little puppy came and sat beside him.

"Hello, little one," said Foley. "Do you have anywhere to go? Will you stay with me?"

She stayed. Foley called her Star.

"This is going to be a great welcome home surprise for Jem," said Foley.

But Jem wasn't thinking about ending his vacation at the moment. Not . . . just . . . yet!